This book belongs to

Child Care

2's Room

An Early Start Edition from Macmillan Book Clubs, Inc.

Amy Loves the Wind

by Julia Hoban

pictures by Lillian Hoban

Harper & Row, Publishers

For my mother

Amy Loves the Wind
Text copyright © 1988 by Julia Hoban
Illustrations copyright © 1988 by Lillian Hoban

Library of Congress Cataloging-in-Publication Data
Hoban, Julia.
  Amy loves the wind.

  Summary: While walking in the park on a windy day,
Amy and her mother see what the wind can do.
  [1. Winds—Fiction.   2. Mother and child—Fiction]
I. Hoban, Lillian, ill   II. Title.
PZ7.H6348Am 1988   [E]   87-45986
ISBN 0-06-022402-9
ISBN 0-06-022403-7 (lib. bdg.)

          1 2 3 4 5 6 7 8 9 10
                First Edition

Amy Loves the Wind

Amy is in the park.

It is a windy day.

The wind chases the clouds across the sky.

The wind tugs
at the balloon man's balloons.

The wind pushes the empty swings.

Does the wind push Amy's swing?

No, Mommy pushes Amy's swing.

Amy goes up high.

Look, there is a pink kite.

It has a bright yellow tail.
The tail dances in the wind.

The leaves dance in the trees.

The wind blows them off.

There is a boy with a bright red cap.

See him chase his cap
across the park.

Will my hat blow away?

No, Amy, your hat is safely tied on.

My hat hugs my head
like my mommy hugs me.